The Brownie KID SQUAD
and the Best Day Ever

A Special Adventure with Zola, The Brownie Girl

CINDY J. CADET
Illustrated By: Ronie Pios

Print information available on the last page

Published by Xlibris 03/03/2016

To order additional copies of this book, contact:
Xlibris
1-888-795-4274
www.Xlibris.com
Orders@Xlibris.com

To my beautiful daughter Abbygail,

I love you beyond words. You are an amazing little lady; you inspire me and bring great joy to my heart/life everyday. May God Continue to bless you and our family for many years to Come!! And a very Special Thank You to my husband and everyone who has supported my dreams and enCouraged me along this journey Called life; your support, prayers, input and kind words mean The world to me, xoxo.

"Mommy, Daddy!" Zola called as she came down the stairs with excitement.

"Good morning, Zola," said Mommy. "How did you sleep?"

"Great," said Zola. "I had the best dream ever last night."

"Really?" asked Daddy. "What was it about?"

Zola sat at the table with her mommy and daddy to tell them about her dream.

"Last night, my best friend Abby, her brother Ethan, my friend Joey, and I met at our favorite playground. I gave them all one of my favorite brownies and told them we were going on an awesome adventure together as The Brownie Kid Squad!

"My best friend Abby really loves to wear tutus because it makes her feel like a princess, so she was wearing her favorite pink-and-purple tutu with glitter on it. Ethan was wearing his lucky red sneakers, and Joey was wearing his special long yellow cape. He loves to act like a superhero. We all had backpacks, except for Joey because he had his cape on; Ethan had some of Joey's things in his backpack.

"We took turns going down this huge golden slide.

"We slid into a magical place called S'more Village. It was so cool. There were colorful hills, pine trees, and an awesome teal path to walk on.

"We decided we would go hiking, camping, and even swimming in the lake. Joey was excited to sleep outside since he had never gone camping before. We sang songs as we tried to figure out where we should build our tent; I brought a green tent for us because green is my favorite color. We even sang a special song about being The Brownie Kid Squad.

"As we were hiking, we saw some bear tracks. Abby was a little afraid we would run into a big bear. Ethan made a roaring noise and told her not to worry, as he would protect all of us. Joey had a map, but we didn't know how to read it, so we just walked around until we found a spot we all thought was perfect. There was a gigantic tree and a rock wall. The spot felt so cozy.

"We were so happy to put down all our stuff. We began to set up the tent together as a team; there were four pegs, so we all dug one into the ground. Abby and I brought flashlights, bug spray, and canteens. Ethan had a first-aid kit in his backpack, and we all had sleeping bags for later. Our stomachs started growling. Even though we all had sandwiches, water, and brownies, Joey wanted to lead the way for us to catch some fish. He thought he was the best at fishing since he always went fishing with his dad at a lake near his house. He secretly had his fishing pole hidden under his cape. It was a special pole that can be folded.

"I put on my bathing suit before we headed to the lake because I wanted to go swimming. Abby said she wanted to swim in her tutu, and Ethan was so hungry he just wanted to stay and eat his sandwich, but we all went to the lake together as The Brownie Kid Squad team that we are.

"Joey showed us how to fish and shared his fishing pole with us, so we all took a turn. Abby and Joey were the only ones who caught a fish, but they threw them back in the water. We didn't want to cook the fish!

I jumped in the lake, and then Ethan jumped in too. Abby and Joey just ran around and chased each other.

"There were three swings near the lake, and we all raced to get on. I got on one, Abby got on one, but Joey pushed Ethan to get on the last swing first. Ethan was mad and yelled at Joey, 'Hey, that's not fair! Why did you push me? I got to the swing first.'

"Joey just laughed and said, 'Don't be a baby.'

"Ethan tried to push Joey off the swing, and Abby started crying and yelling at Joey for pushing her brother. I waved my hands in the air and said, "Come on, guys, we shouldn't be fighting. We should be having fun!"

"Abby said, 'It's not nice to tease people.'

"Joey looked at Ethan and said, 'I'm sorry, I shouldn't have pushed or called you a baby.'

"Ethan just stood there with his arms crossed, and then Joey said, 'Come on, you can get on the swing now, or do you want to race me back to the tent?' Ethan smiled and agreed to race.

"Ethan won the race, and Joey gave him a high-five. Then we changed our clothes, ate our sandwiches, and drank water from our canteens.

"The sun was going down, and we saw someone walking by who helped us start a fire. He told us kids should never start fires by themselves. We made brownie s'mores. They were so yummy; we roasted our marshmallows with sticks and put the gooey marshmallow between a brownie and a graham cracker.

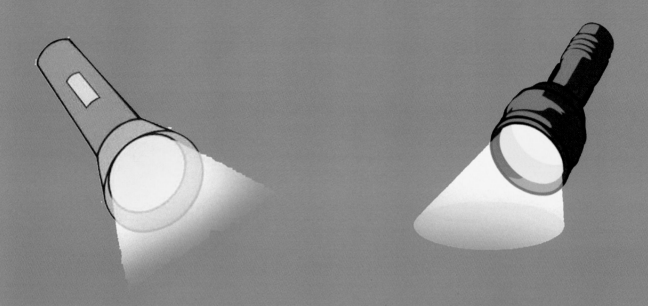

"We set up our sleeping bags and used the flashlights in the dark to make silly faces in the tent before we fell asleep."

"What a nice dream!" said Mommy, and Daddy agreed.

"We should go camping this weekend," said Daddy.

"Hooray! Can I invite my friends?" Zola asked.

"Sure, but we have to talk to their parents first," said Mommy.

The next day Zola was telling her friends at school about the dream and asked her classmates, "Do you want to join The Brownie Kid Squad too? Making a brownie s'more was the way to become part of the squad!

What you need:

Choose one of your favorite brownies (fudgy and gooey are the best)

Pick mini-marshmallows (white or colorful ones), regular marshmallows, or even marshmallow fluff

Graham crackers

Chocolate bars (optional)

What to do:

If using marshmallow fluff, no microwave heating is necessary

1. On a plate, place marshmallow on a graham cracker square.

2. Put the plate in the microwave and heat it on high for ten to twelve seconds or until the marshmallows puffs in size.

3. Remove the plate from the microwave and top the marshmallows with small pieces of chocolate squares (optional) to fit on the crackers.

4. Top with your warm yummy brownie square—sandwiching the filling.

5. Turn over so the chocolate part on the graham cracker is facing upward. Squish together until marshmallow oozes out a bit and chocolate begins to melt!

Yum . . . Time to enjoy!

Send a photo of your best brownie s'more to thebrowniekidsquad@gmail.com and you will be entered into our monthly drawing to win a cool prize. Please visit and LIKE our Facebook page www.facebook.com/TheBrownieKidSquad to get updates and stay tuned for details about our next adventure!

What child doesn't like to have fun? Come join Zola, the Brownie Girl, and the Brownie Kid Squad as they go on an awesome adventure! Zola's friends are cool and unique. You don't want to miss this great friendship experience. They explore, work together, and bond in a very special way.

A family story all readers near or far can enjoy!

Let's come together to help make a difference everywhere. A donation will be made to 2 children charities when you purchase this book.

For more details please visit:
http://www.facebook.com/TheBrownieGirl

Cindy J. Cadet has worked with students in diverse age groups. After obtaining her MBA, she began her journey as a substitute teacher in the classroom with kindergarten children. She then worked in higher education administration.

Cindy, a wife and mother, is very passionate about family life and solutions to building a strong and loving foundation. Being a mom has inspired her to write a fun story about a girl who is smart and adventurous and loves doing new things. Cindy lives with her family in Connecticut.

Xlibris

ISBN 978-1-5144-5814-3

51599

9 781514 458143